D0469242

This book belongs to

_____

Bluebell Glade

Dandelion Dell

Heart of Misty Wood

Hawthorn Hedgerows

Heather Hill

Sundown Hill

Crystal Cave

Golden Meadow

Moonshine Pond

Dewdrop Spring

Honeydew Meadow

Mulberry Bushes

Misty Wood Rabbit Warren

HOME SWEET HOME

How many Fairy Animals books have you collected?

- ❀ Chloe the Kitten
- ❀ Bella the Bunny
- ❀ Paddy the Puppy
- ❀ Mia the Mouse
- ❀ Poppy the Pony
- ❀ Hailey the Hedgehog
- ❀ Sophie the Squirrel
- ❀ Daisy the Deer
- ✔ Kylie the Kitten
- ❀ Paige the Pony

Fairy Animals
of Misty Wood

Kylie the Kitten

Lily Small

Henry Holt and Company
New York

With special thanks to Anne Marie Ryan

Henry Holt and Company, *Publishers since 1866*
Henry Holt® is a registered trademark of Macmillan Publishing Group, LLC.
175 Fifth Avenue, New York, NY 10010
mackids.com

Text copyright © 2014 by Hothouse Fiction Ltd.
Illustrations copyright © 2014 by Kirsteen Harris Jones.
Cover illustration © 2014 by John Francis.
All rights reserved.

First published in the United States in 2017 by Henry Holt and Company.
Originally published in Great Britain in 2014 by Egmont UK Limited.

Library of Congress Cataloging-in-Publication Data
Names: Small, Lily, author.
Title: Kylie the kitten / Lily Small.
Description: First American edition. | New York : Henry Holt and Company, 2017. |
Series: Fairy animals of Misty Wood ; [book 9] | First published in 2014 by
Hothouse Fiction Ltd. | Summary: Kylie's excitement over going to summer camp
with her friends is threatened by her fear of the water. Includes activities.
Identifiers: LCCN 2017028189 (print) | LCCN 2016057766 (ebook) |
ISBN 9781250126993 (Ebook) | ISBN 9781250126986 (pbk.)
Subjects: CYAC: Fairies—Fiction. | Cats—Fiction. | Animals—Infancy—Fiction. |
Camps—Fiction. | Fear—Fiction.
Classification: LCC PZ7.S6385 (print) | LCC PZ7.S6385 Kyl 2017 (ebook) |
DDC [Fic]—dc23
LC record available at https://lccn.loc.gov/2017028189

Our books may be purchased in bulk for promotional, educational, or business use.
Please contact your local bookseller or the Macmillan Corporate
and Premium Sales Department at (800) 221-7945 ext. 5442
or by e-mail at MacmillanSpecialMarkets@macmillan.com.

First American edition, 2017
Printed in the United States of America by
LSC Communications, Harrisonburg, Virginia

3 5 7 9 10 8 6 4 2

# Contents

CHAPTER ONE

Camp Sunshine

It was dawn in Misty Wood.
The sun was just starting to rise,
painting the sky with beautiful
stripes of rosy pink and purple.

Kylie the Kitten lay on her mossy bed, listening to birds chirping in the fir tree overhead. Their sweet songs usually woke Kylie up, but today she was awake long before the birds started to sing.

Kylie jumped out of bed and arched her back, stretching her glittering blue-and-golden wings.

She glanced at her reflection in a little pool of dew. Then she licked her velvety paws and smoothed down her fluffy white-and-ginger fur. Kylie wanted to look her very best today.

"Good morning," Mom purred from the other side of their home in the roots of the fir tree. "Would you

like a honey-and-berry muffin?"

Honey-and-berry muffins were Kylie's favorite breakfast, but this morning she was too excited to eat. It felt like she had a family of butterflies inside her tummy! Kylie nibbled a few bites, and then brushed the crumbs off her whiskers. Padding over to a toadstool, she picked up a little basket resting on top. It was made from woven flower stems.

Most mornings, Kylie used her basket to collect water from Dewdrop Spring. Like all the fairy animals of Misty Wood, Kylie had a very special job to do. Cobweb Kittens like Kylie decorated the cobwebs of Misty Wood with dewdrops so they sparkled in the morning light. But today Kylie was using her basket for something else. She was packing for summer camp!

Every year, the older fairy animal children were invited to spend a weekend at Camp Sunshine. It was the first time Kylie was old enough to go! She'd heard lots about camp from the other Cobweb Kittens. There were teams and challenges and prizes to win. It sounded like so much fun—and best of all, her friends Connie and Chloe were going, too!

Kylie had never spent the

night away from home before. She
suddenly worried that she might
feel homesick at bedtime. Then
she had an idea. She went outside
and fluttered her wings, heading
from tree to tree until she spotted
what she was looking for. Stretched
between two branches of a tree was
a lacy spiderweb. Kylie carefully
took the web down and folded it
neatly. Now she had something to
remind her of home.

"It's almost time to go!" Kylie's mom called up to her.

Kylie fluttered back to where her mother was waiting.

"Do you have any space left in your basket?" Mom asked.

Kylie nodded, holding it up.

Mom popped a few muffins into the basket and twitched her tail playfully. "I know you're too excited to eat now, but you might get hungry later on."

It was finally time to head out.
Kylie and her mom fluttered their
wings and rose into the air.

Below them, Misty Wood
stretched out like a glorious paint

9

palette, its colors shining in the morning light. Everywhere they passed, fairy animals were busy working to make the wood a beautiful place to live.

In Honeydew Meadow, Bud Bunnies were hopping into the sunlight, ready to nudge open the buds of the yellow buttercups. Nearby in the Heart of Misty Wood, Bark Badgers were carving beautiful designs on the tree trunks.

Holly Hamsters were nibbling
patterns into holly leaves, and Moss
Mice were shaping mossy cushions
with their paws.

As they flew over Dewdrop
Spring, Kylie could see the Cobweb
Kittens filling their baskets. They
laughed as they dived in and out
of the glittering fountain, catching
dewdrops that twinkled like
diamonds.

The grown-up Cobweb Kittens

waved to Kylie and called, "Have fun at camp!"

Kylie waved back, but she flew higher in the air to avoid the dazzling jets of water. Although Kylie loved making cobwebs sparkle, she wasn't very fond of getting splashed. You see, Kylie had a secret. It was such a big secret that not even her very best friends knew about it. She was scared of water!

Kylie and her mom flew a bit farther, past a little waterfall and over a glade of trees, and then Kylie's mom said, "Here we are!"

Just ahead of them was Moonshine Pond, shimmering with pearly light. Lily pads dappled the water's surface, and long, fuzzy cattails and pretty blue irises grew all around the pond.

"But this is Moonshine Pond," Kylie said, confused. From the

14

13

name, she'd guessed that Camp
Sunshine was in a sunny meadow.
Oh, dear—this wasn't very good
at all.

"The camp is just there, by
the bank," said Mom. She pointed
toward a row of colorful tents
tucked back from the water's edge.

As Kylie got closer, she saw
that the tents were woven from
reeds, and each one was decorated
with a different flower. Glossy red

15

poppies, bright yellow daffodils, pretty bluebells, and snowy-white lilies all sweetly perfumed the air.

The camp looked lovely, but Kylie felt scared. What if water from the pond splashed her? Or even worse—what if the campers had to go swimming?

"Actually, I think I'd rather stay home," she fretted.

"Don't be silly," her mom said. "You'll have a brilliant time."

16

As Kylie and her mom
landed on the banks of the pond,
young fairy animals were playing
everywhere. Two Pollen Puppies
were wrestling on the ground, while
a fluffy Bud Bunny played tag
with a group of tiny Moss Mice.
A small cluster of Dream Deer
and Hedgerow Hedgehogs stood
giggling together.

Kylie looked around nervously,
but she couldn't see her Cobweb

Kitten friends anywhere. Everyone else seemed to have made new friends already.

She gulped. First there was the pond, and now Kylie was on her own. The butterflies in her tummy returned, but this time they were flying loop-the-loops!

CHAPTER TWO

Acorn Team

A beautiful, pale yellow Petal
Pony trotted over to Kylie, her
shimmering blue wings open wide.
"Welcome to Camp Sunshine!"
she said. "Is it your first time here?"

20

Kylie nodded shyly.

"I'm Poppy," the pony said, flicking her silky mane out of her kind eyes. "I came to Camp Sunshine last summer and had so much fun. You're going to love it here! Come and meet everyone."

Kylie looked over at the other fairy animals nervously. Would anyone want to be her friend?

"Are you feeling shy?" Poppy asked her gently.

21

"A little bit," Kylie admitted.

The pony smiled at Kylie. "That's just how I used to feel," she said. "Not too long ago, I was much too shy to talk to anyone."

But Poppy seemed so friendly and brave. "What did you do?" Kylie asked.

"I learned that if you're kind, everyone will want to be your friend," Poppy said. "And camp is a great place to make new friends."

22

Kylie suddenly felt much better. If Poppy could make new friends, then so could she!

Kylie turned to her mom. "I'll miss you," she meowed, burying her face in her mom's ginger fur.

23

Mom nuzzled Kylie's nose and said, "I know you'll have a wonderful time, my brave girl." Then she fluttered her wings and set off for home.

Kylie and Poppy flew over to the crowd of campers, who had begun to form a circle. Two Stardust Squirrels were also arriving, their bushy tails leaving a shimmering trail of stardust behind them.

"Hurry up, Sally," the older

squirrel called to the younger one, who was scurrying after her. Then she squealed, "Hi, Poppy! Come and sit next to me." She turned to her younger sister. "Stay here, Sally. I'm going to play with my friends."

The squirrel named Sally sat down next to Kylie. A Bud Bunny with soft white fur and spots the color of chestnuts hopped over and sat down on Kylie's other side. Her

whiskers were trembling, which made Kylie think that she might be feeling a bit nervous, too.

Plucking up all her courage, Kylie said, "Hello. I'm Kylie. Is this your first time at Camp Sunshine?"

The Bud Bunny nodded. "I'm Bonnie." Then she added in a whisper, "I was so nervous about coming here that I couldn't eat any clover this morning!"

Kylie smiled and held out her

basket. "Would you like a honey-and-berry muffin?"

Bonnie took one and started nibbling. Her purple eyes lit up. "Yummy scrummy in my tummy!"

Kylie giggled. She liked Bonnie. Her mom and Poppy were right—it was easy to make new friends when you were kind! Kylie asked the Stardust Squirrel on her other side if she'd like a muffin, too.

"Thanks," the squirrel said,

helping herself. "I'm Sally. My
big sister Suzy came to camp
last summer, so I can tell you
everything you need to know."

But before Kylie and Bonnie

could ask her any questions, a
Bark Badger made his way into
the middle of the circle and held
up a strong black paw for silence.
The campers stopped chattering
and listened with respect, for Bark
Badgers were very kind and wise.

"Welcome to Camp Sunshine,"
the Bark Badger said. "I'm Barry,
the camp leader. We have a very
exciting weekend planned for you."

He smiled kindly at the

campers. "But first, let's sing our welcome song. Can the campers who've been here before help me teach the others?"

"Oooh—I know this song already," Sally whispered to Kylie and Bonnie. "My sister taught me."

Barry cleared his throat and began to sing in a deep voice. Poppy, Suzy, and the other older campers chimed in loudly, and before long everyone else joined in.

"We love it at Camp Sunshine

Where the days are long and fine.

We have fun in the summer sun,

Welcome, welcome, everyone!"

When they'd finished singing,
Barry said, "Over the next two days
you'll be working in teams."

I hope I'm on the same team
as Connie or Chloe, thought Kylie,
waving to her Cobweb Kitten
friends. She'd finally spotted them
sitting across the circle.

"This weekend is all about making *new* friends," continued Barry. "So we've put you all on teams with different fairy animals."

Excited chatter broke out. Then Barry picked up a piece of bark carved with names and read out the teams. Poppy the Petal Pony was on Pinecone Team. Chloe was put on Chestnut Team, and Connie on Buttercup Team. More teams were called, but Kylie wasn't on

any of them. Had the Bark Badger

forgotten her?

"And last but not least, we

have Acorn Team," Barry said.

"Petey, Bonnie, Sally, and Kylie."

Kylie and Bonnie looked at each other in delight. They were on the same team! Kylie's tail twitched happily, and Bonnie hopped with excitement.

A brown puppy bounded over and somersaulted to a halt in front of them. Scrambling onto his white paws, he gave a cheerful salute and barked, "Petey the Pollen Puppy reporting for Acorn Team duty!"

Sally the Stardust Squirrel

fluffed out her tail. "The first thing we need to do is pick our tents," she said. "Follow me, girls!"

Kylie and Bonnie scampered after her toward the tents.

"How about this one?" Bonnie suggested, pointing at a tent with delicate sprigs of lavender.

"No, this one's much better," said Sally, hopping over to a tent covered with garlands of bright orange lilies. Without waiting for a

reply from the others, she pushed through the ferns that made the tent's door flap.

Kylie and Bonnie followed her inside. As she looked around, Kylie gasped. The beds were mossy cushions, just like hers at home. But these cushions were stacked on a frame made out of sticks—one on top of the other!

"I'll have this one!" cried Sally, fluttering up to the highest cushion

and wrapping her fluffy tail

around her like a blanket.

Kylie chose the bottom bed.

She padded over and set down

her basket. Then she took out her

37

cobweb and spread it carefully over her moss cushion.

"What's that?" Sally asked, looking down and frowning.

"It's a cobweb," explained Kylie. "To remind me of home."

"I think it's pretty," Bonnie said.

"We don't need a boring old cobweb to make this tent pretty!" cried Sally. "I've got a much better idea." She leaped down from the top bed and spun around in circles. Her

tail shook out a flurry of stardust,
making the whole tent shimmer.
It did look very pretty, but Kylie
couldn't help feeling a little hurt.
She didn't think that cobwebs were
boring at all.

Just then, Poppy poked her
head around their door flap. "Don't
get too comfy, girls," she said,
laughing when she saw them in
their beds. "The first game is about
to begin!"

40

CHAPTER THREE

Woodland Treasure Hunt

Kylie and her teammates scampered outside. Along with Petey, who was sharing a tent with a Dream Deer

and a Hedgerow Hedgehog, Acorn Team made their way to Barry.

"The first fun activity is a Woodland Treasure Hunt," he told the campers. "It's a great test of speed and teamwork. Each team must find five different woodland treasures. The first team to return with all five will be the winner."

Barry handed Kylie a piece of bark with their instructions. Petey, Bonnie, and Sally huddled around.

"We need to find an oak leaf and a twig," Kylie said, pointing at the beautiful pictures Barry had carved with his sharp claws.

"Ooh! And some moss and a daisy," Bonnie said.

"And a big stone, too," Petey added.

Kylie was relieved that they didn't have to bring back any dewdrops from Dewdrop Spring.

"Easy peasy summer breezy,"

Sally said. "I know where to find all those things!"

Kylie glanced at the other teams, who were studying their lists and murmuring quietly. "Maybe we should make a plan first," she suggested shyly.

But Sally was too busy jumping up and down and cheering. "We are Acorn Team, so shake your furry tail! We are Acorn Team and we will never fail!"

Petey's tail wagged so fast it looked like a blur! Bonnie was hopping up and down, too.

Then Barry clapped his hands and called, "Have fun and remember to work together." He tooted loudly on a reed flute and the Woodland Treasure hunt began!

"Shall I get my basket?" Kylie asked the others. "It might be handy for carrying our treasures."

"There's no time for that,"

45

cried Sally. "Let's go!" She opened her wings and flew up into the air. Petey and Bonnie followed after her, their wings sparkling like rainbows.

Not wanting to be left behind,

Kylie beat her wings as quickly as she could. "Where should we go first?" she asked breathlessly.

"To the Heart of Misty Wood, of course," ordered Sally. "That's where I gather acorns. There are lots of oak trees there."

The midday sun warmed their backs as they flew to the very center of Misty Wood. Trees spread out beneath them like a sea of green. Kylie and her new friends

47

fluttered down to the ground. It was much cooler here, deep in the woods. The leaves overhead rustled in the breeze.

"This is lovely," Petey panted, rolling around on the soft ground.

"We don't have time to play," said Sally bossily. "We need to find an oak leaf."

"I see one!" cried Bonnie, hopping over to a big tree. She came back waving a green leaf.

"Yippee!" called Kylie. "We've got the first treasure on our list!"

Petey ran into the woods for a moment, and came back with a twig in his mouth. He dropped it at their feet with a flourish. "Here's the second treasure!"

"Hooray!" Kylie and Bonnie cried together.

"I've spotted something, too," Sally said. She scampered over to the oak tree's trunk, where its thick,

twisty roots grew out of the damp soil. She scooped something up in her paws, and came back holding a velvety pile of moss. "That's the third thing," she said proudly.

"So what's next?" Petey asked.

Kylie checked. "A daisy."

"I know where there are lots of daisies," the Pollen Puppy yelped. "Just follow me!"

Team Acorn rose into the air again. As they flew over Moonshine

Pond, Kylie glimpsed the row of colorful tents. None of the other teams had returned yet.

"Hurry, team!" cried Sally.

The Golden Meadow stretched in front of them, its green grass dotted with yellow buttercups and dandelions.

Petey dived down and tumbled into a bed of dandelion clocks, scattering fluffy white seeds everywhere. "Whee!"

51

The long green grass tickled Kylie's tummy as she landed on the meadow. Nearby, a group of Pollen Puppies were frolicking, wagging their tails and sending up clouds and clouds of fluffy pollen so that new flowers could grow.

"Hi, everyone!" Petey called to the Pollen Puppies. "Have you seen any daisies?"

A white Pollen Puppy with a black patch over one eye pointed

52

across the meadow. "Try over there,
just past that patch of clover."

Kylie and the others dashed
across the meadow after Petey,
whose long ears streamed out

behind him. Then he came to a sudden stop and they all tumbled over him into the grass.

"Oops-a-daisy," joked Petey.

Kylie stood up, laughing. They were surrounded by green stalks topped with small, round buds.

"Oh no," Petey said, his laughter turning to dismay. "The daisies haven't bloomed yet."

Oh, dear, thought Kylie, biting her lip. Sally looked *very* annoyed.

54

"I'm sorry," whimpered Petey. "I really thought we'd find a daisy here."

"You've forgotten that there's a Bud Bunny on your team," Bonnie reminded him. Hopping over to the daisy buds, she nudged them gently with her twitching nose.

"Ta-da!" she said. As if by magic, the buds started to unfold, one white petal at a time. Then the flowers lifted their yellow faces

up to the sun and bobbed joyfully in the breeze.

"Wow!" Kylie breathed.

"It's just what we Bud Bunnies do," Bonnie said modestly. Then she picked a daisy and tucked it behind her long, silky ear. "What's the last treasure we need to find?"

"A big stone," Kylie replied.

Everyone thought hard. Where, oh where, could they find a big stone?

"I've got it!" cried Kylie. "There are lots of big stones around Crystal Cave."

"That's not far from here," said Petey. With a flurry of beating wings, the fairy animals flew toward the Crystal Cave. Soon Kylie could see the crystals inside twinkling like fairy lights.

"Kylie was right!" shouted Petey. "There are lots of big stones."

The fairy animals landed just

outside the cave. Grunting with effort, Petey picked up a big stone. "If you take the twig, Kylie, I'll carry this."

But when Petey fluttered his wings, nothing happened. He tried again, beating his wings harder. Still he stayed on the ground.

"What's wrong?" Sally asked, frowning.

"The stone's too heavy," Petey gasped. "I can't fly with it."

"Let me try," Sally said. "I'm very strong." She picked up the stone and fluttered her wings—but it weighed her down, too.

"If only we'd brought Kylie's basket along," Bonnie said sadly. "We could all help carry it."

That gave Kylie an idea. Without stopping to explain, she dashed into Crystal Cave. It was dark and spooky inside. Kylie felt along the rough walls until she

59

found something soft and silky. Gathering it up, she ran back toward the sunlight.

"A cobweb?" said Sally rudely, when she saw what Kylie was holding. "How's that going to help?"

"Cobwebs look delicate, but they're actually very strong," Kylie explained. She spread the cobweb on the ground and placed the stone right in the middle. Then she laid the leaf, the twig, and the moss next

to it. "If we each take one corner of the web, we should be able to fly our treasures back to camp."

Everyone picked up a corner. "On my count," Kylie said. "One . . . two . . . THREE!"

The fairy animals fluttered their wings furiously and rose into the air, lifting the cobweb along with them.

Kylie held her breath. Would the cobweb hold?

It sagged in the middle, but the web held strong as they flew with their treasures back to Camp Sunshine. They landed on the banks of the pond and then sprawled on the ground, panting.

"Well done, Acorn Team," said Barry as he came over to greet them. "What a clever way to carry your treasures."

"Did we win?" Sally asked him breathlessly.

"I'm afraid not," Barry said kindly. He nodded at the pond, where Suzy, Connie, and two other fairy animals were splashing in the water. Team Buttercup had won the treasure hunt!

CHAPTER FOUR

Showtime

"I expect you're hot after all that hard work," Barry said, seeing the disappointment on Acorn Team's faces. "So why don't you cool

off with a nice dip in Moonshine

Pond?"

"Come for a swim, Sally," her

sister called. "The water's lovely!"

"Time for a doggy paddle!"

barked Petey, bounding toward

the pond.

"Last one in is a stinky

toadstool!" Sally cried, chasing

after him. Soon most of the

campers were splashing in the

water. But Kylie hung back.

"Don't you want to go
swimming?" Bonnie asked her.

Kylie didn't want to tell Bonnie
her secret. Her new friend seemed
kind, but Kylie was afraid she'd
laugh. It was silly for a Cobweb
Kitten to be scared of water!

Kylie looked over at the other

campers playing in the pond. Sally
and her sister were floating on their
backs, their tails spread underneath
them like fluffy rafts. Poppy the
Petal Pony was letting a little Moss
Mouse and a Holly Hamster slide
down her long neck and splash
into the water. Petey was clowning

around, wearing a lily pad on his head. Everyone was having so much fun. But even the thought of dipping her paw in the water made the butterflies in Kylie's tummy come back.

"Er . . . my tummy hurts a bit," Kylie said.

"You poor thing!" Bonnie exclaimed. "I'll keep you company."

Kylie and Bonnie stretched out under a weeping willow tree. They

68

gazed up at the blue sky dotted
with clouds as white and fluffy as
Bonnie's tail.

"Why don't we look for pictures
in the clouds?" Bonnie suggested.
She pointed her paw up at the sky.
"See! There's a fish."

Kylie tilted her head and
squinted at the cloud. It *did* look
like a fish. What a fun game! She
stared up at the sky and suddenly
saw lots of interesting shapes. "Ooh!

That one looks like a pinecone. And that one looks like a hedgehog balancing on a toadstool."

The rest of the afternoon flew by. When the sun had dipped lower

in the sky, Barry called the campers
over for their dinner.

Kylie's eyes grew wide when
she saw the feast laid out on a big
old tree stump. There was wild
mushroom medley, watercress
salad, a big pile of hazelnuts, and
heaps of plump, juicy blackberries.
It all looked wonderful!

Kylie and Bonnie filled their
acorn bowls to the brim and sat
down with Petey and Sally around

a toadstool table. Mmm—it tasted delicious! Kylie finished every bite of her dinner, and still had room for a big bowl of blackberries.

A full moon shimmered overhead. Stars twinkled against a velvet sky and fireflies swirled through the night air like sparklers. Owls hooted softly and crickets chirped, singing Misty Wood to sleep with their lullabies. But the campers weren't ready for bed yet.

"Now for our next activity! We're going to put on a talent show," Barry said. "Each team will work on an act, and the team that gets the loudest applause will win."

Acorn Team huddled together.

"I can dance!" said Bonnie.

"And I can juggle," Petey said, picking up three hazelnuts and starting to juggle them.

Sally plucked the hazelnuts out of the air and popped them in her

73

mouth. "I've got a better idea," she said. "We'll put on a play."

"What will it be about?" asked Kylie.

Sally thought for a moment. "It will be about a beautiful and clever Stardust Squirrel who dances in the moonlight. I will play the Stardust Squirrel, of course."

"Who will the rest of us be?" asked Bonnie, disappointed.

"Hmm," said Sally. "Kylie and

Bonnie, you two can be trees. And Petey, you can be . . . the moon."

They started practicing their play. Sally told everyone where to stand and what to do. Then, as Sally pranced about and said her lines, Kylie and Bonnie waved branches in the air, pretending to be trees. Kylie swayed and tried to look treelike, but wished she had a bigger part.

Petey was supposed to stand

still and look serious, but he kept humming a lively tune and chasing his tail. *"Clap your paws and make a sound,"* Petey sang under his breath. *"Find a partner and spin them around."*

"Stop it, Petey!" Sally said crossly. "We won't win if you don't do what I tell you."

"But it's boring," whined Petey. "You're the only one who gets to do anything interesting."

"Maybe we should try

something different," suggested Bonnie.

"Like what?" asked Sally, sulking.

"I know!" said Kylie. "We can all perform Petey's song together."

Even Sally had to agree it was a good idea. They had just enough time for a quick rehearsal before Barry called everyone back together. It was showtime!

Chestnut Team was the first

77

to perform. They had written a
sweet poem about Camp Sunshine
and recited it together. After that,
Buttercup Team did a comedy
routine, with every team member
telling a funny joke. Kylie laughed
so hard that her sides ached.

Pinecone Team was on next.
They did a breathtaking flying
display, turning loop-the-loops
and zooming around upside down.
For their finale, they all flew in

a perfect V-shaped formation
with Poppy the Petal Pony at the
center. Kylie thought she looked
beautiful, as her blue wings
glittered in the moonlight and her
silky tail fluttered in the breeze.
When Pinecone Team finished with
dramatic nosedives to the ground,
the applause was deafening.

After a few more acts, it was
finally Acorn Team's turn. Kylie
squeezed Bonnie's paw for good

luck as they nervously waited for
the music to begin.

Petey started them off, beating
out a rhythm on an acorn drum.
Then Sally joined in, playing a
lively tune on reed pipes. Kylie and
Bonnie danced in time to the music
as they all sang Petey's song:

"Clap your paws and make a sound,
Find a partner and spin them around.
All the fairy animals sing along now—
Doo-bee-doo, then BOW-WOW-WOW!"

Kylie and Bonnie whirled

around faster and faster. Every

time it came to the chorus, they

bowed to each other and spun

around the opposite way. The

audience clapped along happily to the music.

When the song was over, Acorn Team bowed and basked in the applause. Kylie could see her friends Connie and Chloe cheering loudly. The crowd had clearly enjoyed their act, but was it enough to win?

Kylie held her breath as Barry read out the results.

"It was close," he said. "Acorn

82

Team's song got a very loud cheer,
but the winner of the talent show
is . . . Pinecone Team!"

"Oh, conkers and cobwebs,"
muttered Sally. "Second again."

Kylie shrugged and smiled at
her team. "I still had fun."

As Poppy and her team
proudly took another bow, a pale
figure drifted overhead, casting a
long shadow over the performers.

Kylie glanced up. "What's

83

that?" she asked, pointing at the

spooky shape.

"I don't know," Bonnie

whispered nervously.

"Eek!" shrieked Sally. "It's a

ghost!"

CHAPTER FIVE

Morning Glory

Kylie gasped as the spooky figure
hovered in the air. Could it really
be a ghost? She and Bonnie and
Sally clung to one another in fright.

85

But then Suzy laughed. "Don't be so silly," she said. "It's just a Moonbeam Mole."

Kylie peeked past Bonnie and saw a Moonbeam Mole flying over the pond. He tipped out his net and scattered glittering moonbeams over the water. They bobbed on the surface, making gleaming, pearly ripples. It was lovely!

The campers called hello to the Moonbeam Mole, who gave them

a friendly wave in return. Then he
flew away again, his silvery wings
twinkling.

"If the Moonbeam Moles have woken up and started their work, it must be time for us to go to bed," Barry said. "Come on, kids."

"But I'm not even sleepy!" Petey protested with a stretch and a big yawn.

As the pond's dark water shimmered in the moonlight, Kylie headed back to the tent with Bonnie and Sally. Her new friends fluttered to their beds, and Kylie curled up

on her mossy cushion, snuggling
under her cobweb blanket.

"Nighty-night," Sally called
softly from the top bed.

"Sleep tight," whispered Bonnie
from the middle bed.

But Kylie fell fast asleep before
she could even reply.

Kylie was having a lovely dream
about dancing under a starry sky
with a Moonbeam Mole. They were

scattering moonbeams all over Misty Wood, twirling faster and faster until—

"Wakey, wakey, sleepyhead," called Sally. "Time to rise and shine."

Kylie opened her eyes and looked around the tent. Where was she? Then she smiled. It was her second day at Camp Sunshine!

Kylie licked her paws and quickly washed her face. Then she

and the girls stepped out of their tent into the glorious early-morning sunshine. They joined the other campers for a tasty breakfast of seedy loaf and rosehip jam washed down with cups of acorn milk.

"I hope you all slept well," Barry said with a smile. "Today each team will be making something very special."

"I wonder what it will be," Bonnie said.

"I bet we'll be weaving baskets," Petey guessed. "Or maybe Barry will teach us wood carving. You can make a picture of me if you like!" He stood on his hind legs, wagged his tail, and stuck out his long pink tongue.

Kylie and Bonnie giggled. Petey was *so* funny!

"Don't be silly," Sally said, rolling her eyes. "We're camping, so I'm sure we'll be making tents.

My sister went here *last* year, remember."

But Sally and Petey were both wrong. After breakfast, Barry gathered the campers by the side of Moonshine Pond. "Today you'll be making boats," he revealed with a smile.

"Yay!" shouted Petey. "I've always wanted to go sailing!" He danced a wild sailor's jig.

But Kylie suddenly felt very

93

cold. Oh no! She definitely did *not* want to go sailing!

To her relief, Barry explained that they wouldn't be sailing the boats themselves. "Each team will make a model boat, and at the end of the day you'll race them on the pond," he said.

Kylie let out a breath. She could be brave enough to go *near* the pond, as long as she didn't have to go *on* it!

"Right, let's get started," said Sally, rubbing her paws together. "Acorn Team has *got* to win today!"

"Maybe we should plan our boat first," Kylie said. She picked up a twig and started sketching a boat in the thick, oozy mud at the edge of the pond.

"That's a waste of time," Sally said impatiently. "I already know how to make a boat. Come on!"

"Aye, aye, captain," Petey said,

and the rest of the team followed the trail of sparkling stardust from Sally's tail. Kylie followed, too, but Sally's bossiness *was* starting to annoy her a bit.

Sally led her teammates to a grove of trees. "Find as many sticks as you can," she ordered them.

Bonnie and Kylie scampered to and fro, gathering up twigs in their paws. Petey dragged bigger sticks over in his mouth.

96

Soon there was a big pile by Sally's feet. She started to weave the sticks and twigs together into the shape of a boat. The others

tried to help, but Sally shooed them away. "Fetch me some nice long grass," she said.

"Fetch this, fetch that," Petey grumbled as they plucked the longest blades of grass they could find.

"I thought puppies liked to play fetch," Kylie joked, but secretly she was glad she wasn't the only one who thought Sally was being bossy.

When they returned with the grass, Sally used it to tie the twigs together. Kylie looked on, wishing she could help.

"There! It's done," Sally announced, sounding pleased with herself. "Now let's test it out."

Kylie and her team carried the boat back to Moonshine Pond. It was surprisingly heavy.

With a big heave, Sally pushed the boat into the water. But instead

of sailing away, it just bobbed on
the surface.

"Why isn't it moving?" Sally
muttered.

"Er, it *is* moving, Sally," Petey
said. "Just not the way we want
it to."

They looked on in horror. The
boat was slowly sinking into the
pond! Down, down, down it went,
until finally it vanished underwater.
A few bubbles floated to the

surface and then—*pop!*—they were gone, too.

"Oh no!" Sally wailed.

"Don't worry," Bonnie said, giving Sally a hug. "We have plenty of time to make another boat."

"And we'll *all* help," Kylie said, smiling at Petey.

This time, Acorn Team sat by the pond and planned their boat before they started building it.

"The way Sally tied the twigs

101

together was very smart," said
Kylie.

"But maybe it should be
lighter," suggested Bonnie.

They all gathered more twigs.
This time Sally collected lots, too,
and they soon had plenty. Everyone
helped to build the boat, trying out
different designs until they decided
on the best shape.

"I've got an idea," Petey said.
He splashed into the pond and

paddled over to a cluster of lily pads. Petey put the lily pad on his head and swam back to shore with it flopping into his eyes.

Is Petey being silly again? Kylie wondered.

Sloshing out of the water, Petey carefully pressed the big, round lily pad into the boat. "This will be a waterproof lining," he explained.

"Clever!" Kylie said, helping to smooth it down.

"Now we need a mast," said Bonnie.

Petey dragged a long stick over, and Sally tied it to the middle of the boat. Bonnie picked a morning glory vine and wound it around the mast. Twitching her nose against the vine, she nudged its flowers open until the mast was wreathed in blue blossoms.

But the boat still needed a sail. Kylie had an idea. "I'll be right back!"

She quickly flew to her tent
and scooped up her lacy cobweb.
Then she flew back to the boat and
carefully tied it to the mast. There
were still drops of water glistening
on the lily pad lining, so Kylie
sprinkled them onto the sail as a
finishing touch.

Then she and the others
stepped back to admire their boat.
It was sleek but sturdy. The lacy
cobweb sail billowed gently in

106

the breeze, and the drops of water twinkled like crystals in the sunshine.

"It's beautiful!" breathed Kylie.

"Let's go test it out," Petey suggested.

But it was too late. The other teams had all gathered around Barry. The race was about to begin!

CHAPTER SIX

The Boat Race

Acorn Team carefully carried their
beautiful boat to the pond. A light
breeze ruffled the sparkling water. It
was a perfect day for a boat race!

The other teams' boats were wonderful. Poppy's Pinecone Team had obviously been inspired by their name. They'd built their boat from fir cones glued together with sticky pine sap.

Chestnut Team had made their boat from silvery birch bark. Its green sail was a quilt of leaves, daintily stitched together with grass.

Buttercup Team's boat had

the most unusual design. Two
small logs floated on the water,
and a raft made from sticks rested
between them.

Still, Kylie thought that Acorn

Team's was the most beautiful by

far. She crossed her paws for luck.

Barry licked his paw and held

111

it up to see which way the wind was blowing. "Ahoy there, campers! On my signal, you'll launch your ships." He pointed his paw to the bank of the pond beneath the willow tree. "The first boat to land on the other side of the pond will be the winner."

The teams readied their boats. Petey tinkered with the lining, and Kylie made sure the cobweb sail was still firmly attached. The

cobweb was as light as a feather,
but Team Acorn knew how strong it
really was.

"We've just got to win," Sally
said. She shook her tail and gave the
boat a sprinkling of stardust for luck.

Kylie hoped the lucky stardust
would work—and that their boat
wouldn't sink this time. If only they'd
been able to test it. . . .

"Anchors aweigh!" cried Barry,
and the race was on!

Bonnie, Petey, and Sally waded into the pond, but Kylie hung back. She didn't want to get too close to the water. She watched anxiously as her friends gave the boat a gentle push.

The beautiful boat bobbed in place for a moment. Kylie held her breath. Would it float?

Yes! It sailed away, gliding over the rippling water, and quickly took the lead.

"Yay!" Sally cried. "Let's go to the finish line so we can watch it win!"

Kylie hesitated. What if the boat got into trouble and they weren't there to help? "Shouldn't we wait a bit?" she said.

"Don't be such a worrywart," Sally said. "Come on, we don't want to miss the finish!"

Sally took off across Moonshine Pond. Bonnie and Petey flitted after her. All around Kylie, excited fairy

115

animals were making their way to the other side.

Kylie was about to follow when she noticed that their boat had tilted to the side and changed its course. It was heading straight toward a patch of reeds!

"Wait!" she cried, but the others were already off.

Kylie watched in horror as their lovely boat sailed right into the reeds. Soon it was hopelessly

tangled in the long, marshy grasses.

In the distance, Kylie could see Bonnie, Sally, and Petey heading to the finish line. But their boat would never get there if it stayed stuck! Kylie knew she couldn't let that happen.

Gathering all her courage, she opened her wings and rose into the air. She flew to the patch of reeds and hovered over the boat.

Fluttering her wings furiously so that she wouldn't fall in the water, Kylie reached down and gave the boat a nudge, but it didn't move. She pushed it again, harder this time, trying not to get wet. Still the boat was stuck fast.

By now the other boats were already halfway across the pond.

"Help!" Kylie cried. "Acorn Team!" But all the fairy animals were at the other side of the

118

pond, and their cheers drowned out Kylie's desperate cries.

Kylie thought about her teammates waiting for the boat that would never get there. They had worked so hard and this was their last chance to win a prize at Camp Sunshine. As the boat struggled to break free of the reeds, Kylie's heart sank.

There was only one thing to do—but was she brave enough?

She took a big gulp of air and
squeezed her eyes shut. She *could* do
it. She had to.

Then she dived into the water!

A moment later, she came
spluttering to the surface, her eyes
opened wide with surprise. The
water felt slippery and . . . *lovely*!
Moving the reeds out of the way,
she gave the boat a big push, and it
sailed free.

Kylie paddled her paws until

she reached the side of the pond.
Then, after clambering out, she
flew over to the finish line.

"Why are you all wet?" Bonnie
asked.

"Our boat got tangled in some reeds," Kylie said. "But I got it out."

Their boat was moving swiftly across the pond now, its cobweb sail blowing in the wind. It had nearly caught up to the other boats.

"Come on, little boat!" cheered Bonnie.

It cruised past Buttercup Team's boat.

"You can do it!" shrieked Sally.

It glided past Pinecone Team's boat.

"Almost there!" barked Petey.

But Chestnut Team's boat was just too far ahead. It cruised to the finish line first. Chestnut Team cheered and hugged each other. Moments later, Acorn Team's boat reached the finish line, in second place once again.

"I'm so sorry," Sally said, her voice trembling. "I should have

listened to you, Kylie. If we'd all

been there to help you, we might

have gotten the boat free sooner

and won." Tears glistened in her

124

eyes. "I was being bossy again. Just like my big sister always bosses *me* around."

"It's okay," Kylie said, giving her a hug. "We still did really well. You should be proud that we finished second!"

"If it wasn't for your quick thinking, we wouldn't have finished at all." Sally sniffled.

When all the boats had finished, Barry gathered the

campers for the end-of-camp prize-
giving ceremony. "Have you all
had fun?" he asked the campers.

Kylie and the other campers
shouted, "Yes!" and cheered loudly.

First, Barry presented
Buttercup Team with the Treasure
Hunt award. On a piece of bark
he'd carved a beautiful picture of
a treasure chest. As Suzy went up
with her team to collect the award,
Sally cheered the loudest. But Kylie

could tell how badly her friend had
wanted a prize, too.

"Don't worry," she reassured
Sally, patting her fluffy back.
"There's always next summer."

Pinecone Team was given
an award carved with stars for
winning the Talent Show. Poppy
trotted up with the other members
of Pinecone Team on her back to
collect their prize.

Finally, Chestnut Team

127

bounded up to receive their prize,
which was carved with a picture
of a boat. Kylie clapped her paws
together and cheered for all the
winners. It would have been nice to
win something, but Kylie was just
happy to be there. She could hardly
believe it was nearly time to go
home.

But to her surprise, Barry held
up another award.

"And now, for a very special

prize," he announced. "The Camp
Sunshine Team Spirit award goes to
four of our newest campers. Over the
past two days, this team has learned
how to work together—even when
it wasn't easy. Most important,
they've become good friends and
that's what Camp Sunshine is all
about! Congratulations . . . Acorn
Team!"

Sally leaped up and down,
sprinkling glitter from her tail in

excitement. Petey ran around in circles, and Kylie hugged Bonnie tight. Then they all went up to collect a beautiful bark award carved with a smiling sun and a row of tents.

As the other campers cheered, Kylie glowed with pride. Coming to Camp Sunshine was the best thing ever! Not only had she and her new friends won an award, but she wasn't scared of water anymore.

She'd never have to worry about Dewdrop Spring again.

Kylie sighed happily. It was the perfect ending to a perfect weekend. Camp Sunshine was even better than she'd dreamed it would be. She'd made so many friends and had so much fun. Kylie couldn't wait to come back next summer!

Turn the page for
lots of fun
Misty Wood
activities!

Spot the Difference

The picture on the opposite page is slightly different from this one. Can you circle all the differences?

Hint: There are eight differences in
this picture!

Camp Sunshine Word Search

Can you find all
these words from
Kylie's story?

ACORN COBWEB TEAM POND CAMP TREASURE
DAISY SONG BOAT LILY PAD

A	C	O	B	W	E	B	B	P	C	T	E	A	M	D
E	A	D	A	I	S	Y	S	O	N	G	F	H	E	B
A	M	B	D	A	C	O	R	N	E	R	A	E	A	O
O	P	L	I	L	Y	P	A	D	N	O	P	T	E	A
D	A	I	M	P	T	R	E	A	S	U	R	E	I	T